Work
without
Hope

JOHNS
HOPKINS

**Poetry and
Fiction**

*John T. Irwin,
General Editor*

Poems by John Burt

Work without Hope

THE JOHNS HOPKINS UNIVERSITY PRESS

BALTIMORE AND LONDON

This book has been brought to publication with
the generous assistance of the Albert Dowling Trust
and the G. Harry Pouder Fund.

The Johns Hopkins University Press
2715 North Charles Street
Baltimore, Maryland 21218-4319
The Johns Hopkins Press Ltd., London

Library of Congress Cataloging-in-Publication Data
will be found at the end of this book.

A catalog record for this book is available from the British Library.

ISBN 0-8018-5371-0

To Jo Anne

Contents

Work
without
Hope

Prelude

FOR DAVID SUGARBAKER

In the quiet church, before the hymn begins,
I watch the cool shaft slanting to the floor
From narrow windows, unseen high behind me.
Ceaselessly the sparse dust tacks and wheels
Across the blaze whose shape it marks for me,
And winter daylight shimmers in the air:
Brief stars, brief voyagers from shade to shade.
Light falls and falls and I am still alive.

I

The Crickets

FOR JOHN SINCLAIR

You try again to get to sleep again:
You think (although you have no thought) and think;
Time rushes by although it doesn't pass;
You aren't nothing, but are nothing else.
This is how it is, how it will be:
There is a room you lie in, but won't see.

But all along you have been hearing them,
How freely, from their secrecy, they give
Their long sad expiration to the dark.
Again for you, for nobody, they sing,
Who have no hope, but also have no fear:
"We have not gone. We will not leave you here."

Love and Fame

She'd smiled as if she knew him. That kept him up
And scared him some, but more, excited him.
And in the dark, while his brother coughed next door,
He lay awake, wondering about that girl,
Who'd caught his eye just as she tossed her head
To laugh her shy delicious laugh—at what
He never learned—then handed him that smile
And vanished in the intermission crowd
While he just stood there thinking what to say.
That's what it's like. That's what it must be like.
(He hadn't seen it happening to him.)
They look back at you. That changed it all.
But would he ever see that girl again?
His brother coughed and choked. He lit the lamp
And brought a glass of port to still the spasm.
"Just stay a bit, John, won't you?"
                                    "Yes, of course.
I'm wakeful anyway."
                        "Still, I'm sorry."
He wiped the sweaty forehead with the sheet.
"Shh. Go back to sleep. I'll sit awhile."
Would he have the chance to love that girl,
Or any of the girls (or are there any?)
Who might look back at him in just that way?
It was her gift, a secret, like a poem
She might, just from the blue, have handed him
Clear and whole and wholly eloquent
And never to be written, like the rest.
At the window he could count them: one,
Then two, then three drops falling in the dark,

And to the dark, stars swept from the sky
Flashing downward silently all night.
Give me this hour, God, if nothing else.

What Ellen Said

She hadn't said it. What was it she said?

He leaned both hands there, on the sink, and watched
That pale thin face regard him stupidly:
An old man running water from the tap,
As if to fill the cup he wouldn't take.
It had not changed. That disappointed him:
Then nothing ever leaves a mark on me.

The boy, he knew, had drifted back to sleep
In what was still his room, unused awhile.
"She was glad you came," he'd tried to say.
"I'm not sure she saw me."
                              "Yes, she did.
I'm sure she did."
                     "We can't know that, Pop.
I didn't even see her move her lids."
They'd sat an hour. "Pop, let's go to sleep,"
He'd said at last, like talking to a child,
"There's nothing we can do now anyway."
"I'm O.K. You sleep. I won't be long."

The faucet spluttered. Across the hall she lay
As he had left her, in her little room.
That night, before he'd called the boy, he'd asked
Again and again, "Ellen, are you there?"
Her eyes were closed. He knew she was awake.
"Ellen, has it been worth it after all?"
He knew she was awake. She closed her eyes.

"I have to know."

                                                          "Oh, God," she said at last.

And that was it. Later her breathing changed.

He turned the water off. The house was cold.
And nothing happened. Nothing ever would.

Night on the *River Queen*

(PALM SUNDAY, 1865)

"Play 'Dixie,'" he had said, and as the band
Puffed gamely through a tune that once again
They might feel free to like, he saw them turn,
The knot of prisoners beyond the crowd,
The moldy hardtack in their hands, inert.
Poor boys, he thought. They watched him evenly.
Further back, where Richmond was, steam rose
From broken chimneys and from piles of brick.

At last the ship wheezed back into the James
And scooped the muddy current like a teal.
He read aloud: "Duncan is in his grave.
After life's fitful fever he sleeps well."
Later he dreamed, again, he sailed alone,
Swiftly, silently, through dark and fog.

Sapphics

1. Love

Down they all fall; everything growing withers.
Faithful lovers perish before their love does.
When that time comes, you will be nothing to me.
    I will be nothing.

2. Water

Once, and only fleetingly, did I see her
Bend at spring-side, shivering like a willow.
Then she vanished. Still I will drink that water,
    Cool, welling always.

3. Formalities

You were gravely pulling up his best necktie,
Smoothing down his collar for that calm journey.
He drew off the body, a limp, soiled garment,
    With no assistance.

4. A Spring Night

Nightlong branches over me shift in trouble.
I breathe sweet air. Love makes me foolish, hopeful,
Blows me kisses, cold from the mouths of lilies
    Where he is buried.

The Match

Before she'd even reached the sash she knew
It would be nothing. Still, she held her breath.
Maybe. Oh, maybe. The blue trees groaned in sleep,
And the snow was smooth, look how hard she might.
She caught herself, gliding down the stairs:
A disembodied gown, as cool as death,
Pausing at the bend to hear that sift
Of nothing past the door, the muffled yews.
What would it matter? She waited long enough,
And gripped the rail as if to punish it.
Then started back. But in her room again,
Stood at the darkened window like a stone.
So that's it. All right. And then she lit a match.
Out in the wind it might have shown her face
Just as the hardened glass showed it to her.
But she was looking past it, to the dark.
She let the match burn down before she turned.

Barren Season

I. Persephone

River, river, who will come?
Whom will you send to me?
The leaves rain down, and all their shades
Glide up and bend to me.

And every night I come to you
And I am all aflame
And wait all night for nobody,
And beg from you a name.

Do not tell me of his gentleness,
How quietly he will steal
Upon the brittle discontent
I will forget to feel.

That coldest helmsman of the air
Will find no shuddering thing
That waits awash in failing light
For his fanatic wing.

River river, who will come?
Whom will you send to me?
The leaves rain down, and all their shades
Glide up and bend to me.

II. Hades

When I shake the boughs
Dark leaves sift down

In all your veins.
When I comb the light from the sky
The river mist stiffens in your breath.

Little savage, turn away
As all your secrets turn:
As thought and fall, as hope and fear,
And lies and lies and lies,
And last of all
The quiet creeping to the ear of death.

III. Demeter

Where the shadows broke
There I lay down.

The wind was wide awake.
The pale snow lay like thought, like moonlight.

There was a star that opened in your skin,
A mouth that stained your own mouth black.
There was a stranger's gaze
Pressed to your strange gaze.

And all green things are stranger to me now.
I will be cold here in the cold.
The reeds are baffled in the frozen stream.

Mary's Gift

Pale, bone tired, she raised herself on one elbow,
Brushed her damp hair back with uncertain fingers.
There he was. They wiped off the wrinkled body
    Steaming in lamplight.

"Bring him to me." Fitfully twitching, silent,
How he lay, bewildered, his eyes unfocused,
Fumbling till she steered his blue mouth to nipple.
    "Oh, but he's lovely."

In the forest, shivering, one tree waited,
Secret, patient, keeping watch, still a sapling.
Yet the woman, singing to God in nonsense,
    Taught him what love is.

Ice Storm

FOR MARY ANN ZAKRZEWSKI

A fragile ringing all round suddenly
Awaking me, thought-stupid, elsewhere, chill,
My eyes on nothing but my road, my mind
On nothing but that same old thought again,
Then joy, all joy, as if I'd never been
What I would later be. And there they were,
The living branches radiant in ice,
Their sound like motion in the sky, alert,
Their trembling light uncertain in that wind.
It was their life I had again, and would
No matter what, hold hard to me as breath.
Oh, black branches! We are not made for death.

II

The Sandbar

FOR YVONNE EGDAHL

They wore her ankles raw, those shoes.
But for the rocks she'd pull them off.
Retying them, she stooped to see
The glints of mica in the knots,

And saw the sun, beyond the river,
Falling in the grasp of trees.
Impatiently, they shook and clutched
At nothing, threw hands up and cried

Their high gray cry, like birds in wind.
There was a tire (a bitter smell),
Half drowned, and full of blackened sand,
Webbed through with interesting strings.

Down at the mill the whistle blew,
And it was time. And more than time.
The eddy turned a streak of foam;
Beneath it danced a piece of glass,

Blue glass. She clambered to a rock.
The freezing water, as she reached,
Was half a foot too deep, and rasped
Her bare thin arm like storm-blown sand.

Dark dropped from the trees too fast.
(Just one turn more, and then turn back.)
But look: the smooth stream sliding over,
Swept a white full curve of sand,

Brilliant in dark water, shapely,
Still in the tumult, cool and knowing,
Waiting languidly for her.
Nothing would be like it, ever,

So lithe, so beautiful, so strange.

A Small Animal

Winter nights, I'd climb up there to watch
That star-stung light stream endlessly, inhuman
And serene as angels are, a rush of glitter
Vivid, and perfect, and meaningless.
It swept me up, and I was nothing to it.
It swept me up in its cold certainty,
The one not futile thing in all that stir
I would not be a part of;
                              then at my back
A snap. A rush. A clatter of broken twigs:
Something I'd startled, scrambling for its life.
I turned, and barely caught the flash of fur.
Just out of reach it stopped. I almost saw
How wide its nostrils, its ears cocked up, alert,
Its little heartbeat racing crazily.
Poor thing, I thought. Poor stupid eager thing.
Beyond, I saw the streetlights winking aimlessly.
A car, snow-muffled, crept up a distant hill.
And somewhere on a curb, two women stood,
Waiting for nothing all that winter night.
One lit a cigarette despite the wind.
One took two coffees from a paper bag.

Work without Hope

(1946)

If he had heard the slap, he didn't show,
And he was nobody to her, thank God,
(Her little girl tried and tried to catch
Her breath, but couldn't, and since he looked at her,
Clutched a wet red face against her knee)
Still she was shamed, too shamed to be afraid:
Before she'd looked at him she'd popped the latch
As if to make amends for what she'd done.
"Lady, I can rake this yard real good."
He scratched a bleeding knuckle aimlessly
And nodded calmly at the flagrant yard.
She took her time — *he's drunk at ten o'clock* —
And yet he seemed so sure of what she'd say
She felt she was the one left hanging there.
"All right," she said, "two dollars when you're done."
The rake lay on its back behind the house,
And on its hook, the rusting hand-mower
Which she could never lift. He saw that, too.
And then she knew just why he'd picked out her.
The daughter whimpered, running from the room.
What good will raking do? He ought to mow.
And I'm a fool to fail to ask him to.
But he pulled clean and steady, combed the grass,
Working from the fence out to the street
Without a word, without a glance at her.
Where does he sleep? She had to wash a glass
For lemonade. *I should give him beer.*
To give him anything would ease her mind;
But when he saw her standing on the stoop,
The lemonade in hand, he waved her off.

"I'll drink it when I'm done."

                              "The ice'll melt."
"I can't have it till I'm done, I said."
She stared. "I have to work before I eat."
"All right."

                    "I have to walk and find some work.
Then I can eat." This to himself, not her.
Inside the door, she tucked in strands of hair
And watched him heap the rotten leaves in piles.
Then all at once she saw him stop, and bend,
And gingerly, between two fingers, lift
Poor blackened Raggedy Ann out of the leaves.
Just as he dropped her in the trash he saw
That she was watching him. He met her look,
Walked right up to the stoop and propped the rake,
Then slowly, in one swallow, drained the glass.
Then he turned down the walk. "Wait a minute."
But when she came out, fumbling with a bill,
He'd turned the corner. "Wait, God damn it, wait!"
She followed him out to Mount Auburn Street
But stopped: a bus went by, two kids on trikes.
She just couldn't run past all those lawns.
She watched his shoulders work his damp gray shirt.
And then, behind her, finally she heard
The little girl wailing in her room.
Christ. She turned. "I'm coming." *Jesus Christ.*
Later, she looked for him. She looked a week
Before she found him snoring in the dust
Between the river and the Arsenal.
She stood there with the money in her hand.

Common Ground

(OUTSIDE BRIGHAM AND WOMEN'S HOSPITAL)

He knows that kind: you just leave them alone.
But (hell with it) he sits there anyway,
A long way down the bench, though close enough
The boy looks harder, for his benefit,
But not in his direction, pointedly.

He puts as bland a face on as he can.
You don't scare me. And you don't own the bench.
Picture-stiff, he sits. He's had his news,
And Martha, with the car, will have it soon.
That will be harder. He finicks with his tie.
He's proud of that, the tie, the discipline
He will be needing more of, later on.
Fat lot of good that discipline will do.

What's with that boy? He's jigging there in place,
Daring him to steal a glance (he does),
And catching him before he looks away:
He's got a bathrobe on. *Just go ahead,*
He seems to say, *I know you saw it.*
You want to tell that watchman over there?
I'm not bothering you. Leave me alone.
And then he sees the stitches on his throat.
Sweet Jesus Christ. Well, I'm not stopping you.
But someone should have. Someone let you by,
And someone else is on the watch for you
Unless you get there first, you or your friends.

All right, you win. He walks down half a block.
But where is Martha? What is keeping her?

He glances back: a woman with a cane
Is sitting on the bench. Across the street
The boy has met a carful. The driver laughs.
They shake hands in some complicated way.

Thomas Chaplin

November 5, 1850:
Query: is there some knack to married life?
Some magic word my father never told?
Or do all married people live like us?
Consider how, the dinner hour long past,
Miz Mary rises stately from her bed,
A little tired, a little ill, not hungry,
No, not at all, thank you, but might get down
A bite of what she plucks from this noon's lamb
Still squatting in a thickened pool of fat.
Oh but it's tasteless now, she remonstrates,
And heats Eliza up but not the joint.
I can't eat this. How to sustain myself?
And lifting up her skirts sighs back to bed
To eat her griefs, the one thing ever fresh,
And fill her mouth with snuff, and lie amazed,
Drooling from the corners of her lips,
A charming wife, fit for the likes of me.
At dusk she takes a turn about the yard
And eats a cake, quarrels with her "good man,"
And turns the same five pages of her book
All over again, dizzy with her snuff,
But sleepless till past two o'clock each night.
Tomorrow must be better than today.
She must repeat that. So also must I.

Jim Slocum

(1953)

Yes, that's his car all right. Slocum stopped
And fishtailed in the slush just off the road.
Now what's going on? That car is running still.
And burning oil to boot. Just like that boy.
He wiped his misty window with his sleeve.
The car was puffing blue, just twenty yards
Into the dripping thicket, plain to sight
(In daylight, anyway), its windows glazed.
It was a clump of brush, narrow, rain-black,
Between two fields of stubble streaked with ice.
Why would anyone be parked there now?
When Barnett called him, shortly after dawn,
He hadn't thought to look too hard for them.
"You know your daughter's out with Pete Tyree."
(He almost said—he had to bite his tongue—
It's not my fault that you can't run him off.
Maybe she likes him. They're like that, girls.)
"I know he's took her off to Steubenville.
That's why she isn't back."

                "They're man and wife, then."
"Oh no they're not. My girl is under age.
If I catch up to him I'll bust his face."
(And Slocum thought how twenty years ago
He too had crossed the bridge a single man
And come back married, happy for a while.)
"All right. I'll get them. Don't do anything cute."
But then his boy spoke up: they'd been with him
Till ten o'clock, down at the Rivoli.
You don't elope straight from the picture show.
And here the car was, idling in the rain.

But nothing happened when he tapped the glass.
He pulled the door, and there were both of them,
Her head on his bare shoulder, his sheepskin coat
Draped over her back, the collar in her hand.
Her other hand lay softly in his hair.
And both were flushed as if with love, though chill.
You fools, he said aloud, look what you've done.
Just what is love to you two anyway?
You think it's worth this shit? In twenty years
You might be wondering what you saw in him.
You might be glad your father broke it up.
Christ, you might be wishing that he had.
(And maybe that is why they did it now,
Because to have or not is just the same.
No one does and no one ever can.)
It was an accident, he'd tell Barnett.
They left the heater on and fell asleep.
And maybe that was true. He didn't know.
And maybe, drowsy in each other's arms,
It seemed to them like love, he thought that night,
Alone in his narrow bed, his cluttered house,
Love that spent them, love that weighed their limbs
And bound them softly in oblivion,
Love that swept them down and down to dark.

The Stair

Two flights up, behind a locked door,
Someone is playing: Preludes. Then someone
Stops, mid-phrase. You wait for it.
You know how it goes, not how it will go.
The wallpaper is pouring itself into ashes.
In the darkness, one knee bent,
One hand upon the banister,
You are the statue of Ascent.
Some other person climbs into the half-light.
Some other person walks the corridor.
Some other person knocks upon a door.

Travelers

She wiped, again, the breath-mist from the pane,
And shaded the reflection with her hand.
He couldn't see a thing from where he stood
Except his image in the blackened glass.
He stopped himself from asking what she saw.
It's just the traffic, she would say again,
Stiffening, not turning round to him.
One by one, the headlights swept the darkness.
The traffic kept on passing all night long.

III

Aboard the *Californian*

(APRIL 1912)

First the watch cried out, "Ice ahead!"
Then we were in the wan broad maze of light.
The captain brought the engines to full stop,
And said, "No use to pick our way through that.

Tomorrow we head south." He went below.
We were dead in the water, and all around
Were gleaming fields of ice, the honed-steel air,
A broken shimmer flaming in the sky.

Ten miles southeast, another light had stopped.
We fixed on it, no longer so alone,
And wondered who it was. It must have heard:
A signal flare arced up, and then went out.

While we were rolling there, as in a dream,
We saw another flare, and then a third.
Someone woke the captain, and he said
That ship was warning us about the ice.

By four o'clock the light had disappeared.

Viglius Zuichemus

(Dulmen, near Muenster, 12 August 1534)

Dearest and most honored Erasmus:
I trust your pupil has not angered you
By the seven months' delay which now he ends
With all this hurried faulty Latin (whose
Errors I beg pardon for before
They're made); however, on my own behalf
I must submit that far too much has passed
Since last we met for me to tell it all.
You may have heard the rumors which have flown
About this place. And even you, I fear,
Could not make sense of the events (and how
Could I if you could not yourself?). Besides,
I always have expected that this war
Will come at last to some disastrous end,
And when I write to you I ought to have
More pleasant things to say.
                              Well! From your house
I traveled to Cologne; and holed up there
Because of storms, I met a certain learned
Countryman of mine, who offered me
From Franz von Waldeck, Bishop-Prince of Muenster,
A post as secretary to the throne.
Since I was eager anyway to gain
Experience of public life (although
In retrospect I see I should instead
Have edited that Suetonius
You offered me) I had to take the post.

Scarcely did I know what was in store
In that unhappy tempest-brewing town

That reaps the whirlwind it sowed. Hunger
Started it, as usual: the council
Stirred the common folk against the priests
To save their necks (it didn't, by the way),
Then spent themselves, wrangling with each other
As happens when a crown is cast away
In favor of a motley-cap and bells.
Some threw Lutheran inkpots at Old Nick
(They saw him every place but one), while others
Bodied forth new gods from turbid dreams,
But most bent knee to Mammon, being poor.

The Anabaptists have the city now:
One night a defrocked priest, one "Bread Bernard,"
Ran naked through the streets, crying aloud
That all alone he'd wrestled many nights
With evil spirits (as I well believe)
And God Himself had told him to go forth
Into the public ways to choose the saved.
So out they came, tangled in their sheets
No less than their bad consciences, and said
The day of woe will come upon them soon
(Which, no doubt, it will), and beat their heads
Upon the paving stones, tore their hair,
And showed in other ways their perfect faith.
Just after that we brought our armies in.

A certain tailor they have made their king.
He also talks with God, calling himself
The death-angel, and well makes good his boast.

Just bread, says Juvenal, and circuses
Can rule an Empire, but this tailor does
One better: short of bread, thanks to us,
He rules the town with circuses alone.
He parodies the Mass, devises hats,
And with great ceremony disembowels
The luckless wretches he's suspicious of.
He's saved the city from the curse of gold,
I've heard, by taking all of it himself,
And many saintly women come to sing
Hosannas in the highest to his name.
Atop his walls are angels militant
Like none that heaven ever saw.
                                        How strange:
They've fought like Hectors. In another cause
They might have won from us eternal praise.
Our sound and steadfast legions, to speak truth,
Have been not only very slow to fight
But also—it's the way with hired troops—
Not wholly free themselves from novel views.

Each day we beg some local lord for aid,
Who gives us just enough to have a claim
To press upon us when the city falls.
You may hear news before this letter comes.
(Muenster could be ours within the week.)

There's much dissension now among the Dukes
Whether to raze the town or not. Some wits
Advise to leave it be, since after all

So many Anabaptists will be thrown
From off its walls that we should honor it
For service to our cause.
                    Now for myself
I've few complaints. The Bishop is most fair
About my salary, and hints some new
Position shortly may fall in my way.
Time will tell. God knows, my dear Erasmus,
I've paid my dues with all this messy work,
And had some restless nights on its account.
But someone has to do it, and I guess
It might be even worse in other hands.

Elizabeth Keckley

(New York, 1866)

I

I hadn't time to get my breakfast in:
Five-thirty she was pounding on my door,
"Lizzie! Lizzie! This minute, or I'll die!"
And there she was, still wearing last night's dress.
"Good Heavens, miss! Come in."
                                    "Quick! Close the door!"
Then clenched me hard until I lost my breath.
Her hair was musty, and half-alive with knots.
At last I got her settled in a chaise,
And found my brush and thought I'd comb her out.
"Now what's all this?"
                        "Shh! They mustn't hear!"
Then, pointing down. " You've got to whisper, or—"
"Well, keep your own voice down then,"
                                    "*He's* down there!"
"He's in Chicago, miss."
                        "I *heard* him *there.*
He's right down there with Stanton. I heard it all."
"Now what would both of them be doing here?"
"You don't know them."
                        "Shaw, miss. He's your son."
"Oh, that's the shame of it." I put my hands
Across her forehead, and she closed her eyes.
"Oh, that's the shame. If only *he* had died
Instead of—" and she couldn't say his name,
"But I still have my Taddie left, thank God.
I don't know what I'd do if he were gone."
I felt the vessel beating in her face.

"Now you sit still," I said, "You understand?
There is no Robert here, nor Stanton neither."
She slowly drew her breath. "Now sure enough,
I'll go down there myself and haul 'em up.
Who else is down there? Should I make a list?
Why, Stephen Douglas' ghost, and Captain Brown,
And old Jeff Davis, in a woman's dress,
And Mrs. General Ord——"

                         "That whore. Don't name her."

"And Mr. Salmon Chase. And General Grant.
And from the Senate, ten Republicans."
She seemed to sink. "I'm all right now," she said,
"I just was worried that we might be seen."
"We sure will be if you go on this way."
"We have to be so careful. Are you sure
That nobody in Washington will tell?"
"I didn't tell my girls where I've gone.
They like their jobs too much to study me."
"They're always kind to me, the negro girls.
The white folks should be shamed to see themselves."
Shame and whitefolks? Ha, I almost said.
"Well, you can't be too careful, anyway."
"And miss, you watch your temper."

                          "Oh, that scum!
I could have killed that man last night, you know.
Imagine! 'We don't serve Negroes here,' he says.
'Your servant can have supper in the back.'
Right in his piggy face I almost said
'My husband brought the guns from Gettysburg

Straight from the field, to keep your kind in place.'
No wonder they're all Copperheads, the swine.
What will they do with no slaves to look down on?"
"You're *Mrs. Walker* here. You keep that straight,
'Cause *Mrs. Walker* can't boss anyone."
"Well, anyway, we showed him, didn't we?"
I didn't answer. I just bit my tongue:
Like angry poultry we flounced from the room
And made our point, and didn't get to eat.
(And all that day, running here and there,
Breakfast was the last thing on her mind.)
Then up she leapt, both hands in her hair.
"I left the samples down there in my room!"
"Well, then we'll go and get them."

                                 "They'll be gone."
"You hush. There's no thief in New York awake.
Now I'll just straighten up."

                             "No, hurry!"
"You just wait. We can't go out like this.
We look like fishwives. Fishwives don't sell jewels."
"It's just the dresses. I couldn't bring the jewels."
"You mean you brought those dresses here?"

                                 "A few.
The purple velvet, the green silk with the black,
Oh yes, and the gilt brocade."

                             "The gilt. Oh, miss.
You come to sell your dresses secretly
And bring your Inaugural gown?"

                               "All right. I know."
"Why, every paper here engraved that gown.

I got a lot of custom from it too."
"We'll keep it back then. I brought the best of them."
"You should've brought the jewels."
                              "I couldn't do it."
"What will those dresses bring?"
                              "Enough, I hope.
God knows I paid enough to you for them,
And Worth's and Galt's and Woodward's and who else?"
"They won't bring much as Mrs. Walker's clothes."
"They'll have to. That's just it. There's no way else
That I can raise the—how much do I owe?
I can't remember. Thousands, anyway.
No, tens of thousands. It's some genie's curse.
I'll raise it, then I'll owe it all again.
You know, for guns they printed money up,
Just made it up from nothing, lots of it.
And yet they want the President in rags,
Because we're bumpkins, hayseeds, Westerners.
Why, next to Springfield, Washington's a swamp,
A swamp I tried to make a Capital."
I tried to draw her fingers from her hair.
"We'll be all right, miss. Try to catch your breath.
Just let me dress and then we'll get you changed."

II

We looked respectable enough at first,
Or would have, had it not been six o'clock
And no one on the streets except the last

Bedraggled ladies she was frightened of,
Who met our gaze as we could not meet theirs.
She'd pat her hair as if it should be watched
Until despite it all, it got away
And hung a little looser every time
She'd put it back in place. I let it hang.
I knew we'd get there and we'd have to sit
Two glaring hours on that frozen stoop
And by that time she'd pull it all apart.
Maybe at eight I'd get it straight again,
But I was tired, and I just let it go.
"Slow down. You want to break my bones?" I said.
"Oh, Lizzie, we've just got to get there first
So we can get back out again unseen.
Suppose they know us? They've seen my picture, sure,
And it might as well say 'Wanted' underneath
Once people know what we came up here for."
"We'll have to wait. They won't be open yet."
"All right. We'll wait. Don't look at me like that!
I know we'll be a sight, just sitting there,
Don't you think I know as well as you?"
God only knows just what you know, I thought.
"Don't you think I know that? I'm no fool.
All my life I've been somebody's fool.
You think that I don't know just how I look?"
"If you're a fool then I'm another one."
"Oh, I see. You came to set me straight.
You think I need some kind of talking to,
That I can't manage anything alone."
She looked hard at me, calm, not angry yet,

"And maybe you enjoy it, just a bit,
The chance to pick me up and dust me off
Until I'm almost, but not quite, all right.
You like the way I have to cling to you?"
Now this time I was angry: "Miss, be still.
I didn't come up all this way for this."
And then she sighed and drew her jacket close,
And that was that for now: nobody else
Could use that tone of voice with her and live.
"Now tell me, miss, just what you plan to do.
I thought at least we'd bring a dress along."
"That would sure make every tradesman stare."
"Think how they'd stare if they knew who we are."
"Well, that's the point. We have to be discreet."
"Discreet? And talk some man into your room
To look your clothing over?"
                                    "I've a plan."
"Then tell it to me now."
                                    "Oh, Lizzie, no."
"If it's a good plan . . ."
                                    "No, it's just a plan.
There aren't any good plans any more.
You'll try to talk me out of it, I know."
And she was turning round her diamond ring,
But it was tight, almost too tight to budge.
It wore a little groove into her skin.
"I see. You'll show this jeweler your best ring
And bring him to your room to show the rest."
"That way we'll do our business secretly."
"He'll be sure you're working for some thief."

"That's why he'll be discreet."

                                        "Or call the Police."

"You don't know these men the way I do.
They like the dollar. They took enough from me!"
"So you're the thief. And I'm the thief's accomplice.
Pretty role you've brought me here to play!"
"Lizzie, please don't talk me out of it.
I'm counting on you here to give me nerve."
"But miss . . ."

                "I know, I know. It's lunatic.
But what else can I do—go freeze at home,
Get put out on the street by creditors?
You know how to make your way alone
But me, I just can't do it. And I have to."
When first I'd brought her back to Illinois
(She wouldn't go at all, except with me)
She flung out of her bed at half past ten
And realized Taddie hadn't gone to school.
He knew the way to have his way with her:
Oh, she was mean, oh, would she *make* him go?
Until she thought he was so sensitive
She'd have to teach him everything herself.
Down came the picture book. "Now what is that."
"I know what it is!"

                  "But read the word."
"It's just a monkey. Don't you think I know?"
"It's not a monkey. What's that letter there?"
"It's a monkey. See? Right there. A monkey."
"That's an 'A.' Does monkey start with 'A'?"
"I guess it does."

"Well, guess again. What's that?"
He looked away. "Young man, is that a 'P'?"
He took his hand from hers. "Now you're no fun."
"Just tell me what's the word. What's A-P-E?"
"It's a monkey. I told you so before."
By this time it was noon, and Robert came
And carried him by main force off to school.
He's a dark one, she said all afternoon,
That Robert, did he have to be a brute?
And I was thinking what she'd say if she
Had seen my son spell "monkey" A-P-E.
Why was I there? God, what she wouldn't do
If she were left alone.
                    At eight o'clock
The jeweler found us waiting on his stoop
(Caught me straightening her hair, in fact),
A little rodent man, with muskrat whiskers.
He stood three paces off, mustache atwitch,
As if, reared up on hind legs by his hutch,
He'd sniffed some sort of danger in the air.
I kept my head, and talked my way inside,
But she set loose some speech she'd kept in mind
And had him spooked again. I cut her off.
"We have some things to show."
                              "Nice things?"
                                      "You judge."
She tugged the ring until she got it loose.
"We've more of these."
                    "I bet you do," he smiled.
"Now see here, sir . . ."

                 "Shh. Yes, we've more of these.
But you will have to see them privately."
He slipped a hand into a little drawer,
But brought out just a loupe, thank God, and looked
Coolly for a minute at the ring.
"There is a name engraved inside the band . . ."
And then he started. Why didn't she think of that?
He smiled and looked us up and down again.
"I see. Can you come back at six o'clock?
We'll have to do this business after hours."

III

"Oh miss," I told her later, on the street,
"Why did you have to bring that very ring?"
"Well, it's too late now. But here's a plan."
This time she'd kept a cooler head than me.
"We'll have him show the ring just to our friends.
Secretly, just to the most discreet.
And then we'll raise subscriptions up from them.
They wouldn't want a public row, I think."
I sank down on the curb. "Who are your friends?"
But she was gay: "That's just what we'll find out!"
She took my hand. "Now Lizzie, coragio!"
Why did she have to laugh that way? I stood.
"If this is what we have to do, we'll do.
When Willie died—funny, I said his name.
And just like that. Like any other name.
You know I haven't mentioned him since then?

When Willie died, and I took to my bed
And hoped to die, but couldn't get it done,
My husband made me look—it was just dawn—
And there I saw that Saint Elizabeth's
Where he and I were almost fit to go.
But mothers' sons were dying, tens of thousands,
And mothers went on living. They had to live:
Breakfasts needed to be made, hair combed,
Daughters needed to be sent to school.
'Think about them, Mary,' my husband said.
'But their sons died for something. Ours just died.'
'Died for something? We can't know that yet.'
And then he gave it up and walked away.
Maybe I'll be the only one to live.
We can't just die now, and be noble, can we?
I haven't got the knack for glorious death.
Why, it's all before us now, the world,
Because we have to live. It's what we do.
It's something that we'll do on any terms."
What could I do? I had to smile back.
"God only knows what will become of us."
I didn't say a word. I looked at her.

1938

FOR DAVID MURRAY

They had to haul it to the earth with ropes,
The gang of men who brought the airship in
Those last few feet just short of round the world
In record time. That noon they'd put up flags
And built a vantage for the newsreel men,
And the governor himself came to the pier
To watch them warp it down. Was it alive?
It humped itself, prow first, a little up,
And then the tail fins delicately kicked,
And turned a fraction over.
                              "Boys, pull again,
Just one more time. Before the wind comes up."
And each one had a thought.
                              "No, hold it down."
And back through chains of men the straining rope
Sang out like a bowstring shooting home,
And men locked arms around the waists in front.
"Together, boys.
                  For Christ's sake, one more time."
But it was over. First three or four let go,
And then the gang dissolved to save itself,
And who was left, the steadfast foolish, maybe,
Or maybe just the paralyzed from fear,
Or maybe just the last to feel the shudder
As all at once the rest of them dropped off,
Some six or eight, were hoisted into air.
Most of these let go at twenty feet.
But two held on, and the airship, breaking free,
Shot straight up at the sun triumphantly
Beyond all holding on or holding out.

One man, spread-eagled, hit the hangar roof;
The other thrashed and churned down to the trees
As if to swim the air. But neither screamed.
No one watching them recalled a sound.

I do not know, had I been there that day,
That I'd have held—or if I should have held.
I couldn't pull that airship down alone.
But could we all? I don't know even that.
Could I have kept those men somehow in line?
And if I had, might that have killed us all?
I know those men woke nights, despised themselves,
Saw in their dreams those two come crashing down.
By now they, too, are dead; their moral flinch
Is past extenuation, and past blame.

Dead Boy

(1939)

If you find him, sparrows,
Hide him in flowers,
Whether in the forest
Or by the roadside.

Where the soldiers threw him
Broken in pieces
Softly let him lie, with
Earth for his pillow.

Though I never find him
Under the heavens,
Smooth his covers for me,
Leaf fall and snowstorm.

Let his sleep be quiet.
Clouds, hold your thunder,
Though our life, our hope, is
Plowed with him under.

Peace in Our Time

(November 9, 1940)

*The world's little people will remember their debt to an earnest, hopeful,
bravely pathetic old man who held the Four Horsemen of the Apocalypse back
for an indispensable year, while he alone stood guard in the valley of
humiliation, armed only with the grimness of his courage and an ancient,
tattered umbrella.* — A. Powell Davies

Again he blinked there, on the airplane ramp.
Is this a joke? He gripped the same umbrella,
One spoke bent, and glared into the mist.
You have no right to play with me like this.
But there was no one there. *Just answer me.*
I knew what war was: anything but that.
You tell me just what else I should have done.
And nothing answered. So he straightened, struck
The point of his umbrella on the stair.
Don't I still have to do the prudent thing?
Could I lead that man to reason otherwise?
And how else keep from being just like him?
He caught himself shouting into fog,
Stiff and ridiculous, an angry sparrow.
What do you want? I bought the world a year.
I had no choice. He would have beaten us.
The fog thickened, and his face, like week-old snow,
Grim, and damp, and barren, and amazed
Hardened and paled, and he stood there shaking.
I just don't understand. I did my best.
And yet you punish me for decency.
For God's sake, are you on that man's side?
I will not understand you. You hear? I won't!

IV

Anna Peterson

(Ashfield, Massachusetts, February, 1849)
for Rhys and Eleanor Williams

I

As Hunter sat, propping with his fists
His ugly head, his face turned toward his host
As if attentive, letting him go on,
Moving just his eyes to match the restless
Many-angled pacing of the man
Who spoke too quickly to be grasped, his voice
Tense, high-pitched, unreal, a rusty creak
The man himself would not have recognized,
He gathered almost none of what he heard.
His feet were hurting him; his hands were strange,
Stinging from the frost (the scarlet claws
Of a decrepit scavenger, he thought).
His host was waving a daguerreotype,
As if to threaten someone never seen
Who mocked and laughed and poked him when he turned,
And Hunter saw the candles flash on glass
But not the picture he would have to paint,
Which, just now, wouldn't matter anyway.
The fire was nice, and nicer still the deep
Enfolding plush of the upholstery,
From which he'd never heave his bulk again
If it were up to him. He'd have a drink
He thought, before he started, and his hand
Would be more supple for awhile. A stool
To sit on as he worked, he must remember.
His host marched on, unused to his own voice,
His intonation stumbling up and down,
Snagging sometimes, hanging on a vowel,

Then rushing onward with redoubled speed.
What *was* his name? A Dutchman, Hunter thought.
He rummaged in the dark, then drew it up:
The dry goods merchant, Christian Peterson,
Who'd burst into his room down at the inn
Before he'd even opened his valise,
And canceling the meal he'd just bespoken
(And had been hungry for since yesterday),
Had clutched all Hunter's things in one grim hand,
And with the other towed him through the gale,
Splashing in the slush with skinny feet,
Already giving orders urgently,
And only halfway down the blustery street
Remembering that he hadn't said his name,
Or that he'd waited almost twenty months
To find a traveling painter in his town,
Or what his business was, or where they'd go,
Or half a dozen other things the blast
Had garbled as it rushed past Hunter's ears.
Hunter had panted, his feet, in soaked-through boots,
Grotesque and lifeless, bales of sodden hay.
At last they stopped and stamped before a house
That seemed too big for such a little man,
And Hunter sat and tried to warm his hands.
"It *didn't* look like her, the daguerreotype,"
The man went on, "by God, it isn't her,
That deadness in the eyes, the rigid neck,
Those colorless taut lips, like gutta percha,
That's not my girl at all. It's someone else."
They always look like startled mannequins,

Thought Hunter, who could tell without a glance
Just what was wrong with the daguerreotype.
"Sometimes I just can't bear to look at it.
She's not a stranger. She's not anyone.
She's just some clothing and a formal pose.
But when I sit alone and call her up
I don't see her; I see that picture there."
And Hunter thought, coloring with shame,
How many times *he'd* brought a portrait in
Of nobody (he kept them in his trunk),
And sketched in someone's features in an hour,
Then spent the evening, eating dinner there,
Modeling the cheeks, the liquid eye,
The over-rosy blush they'd want to see.
Each burgher's wife wore black, had folded hands
(He'd never mastered hands), sat in the shade.
He had a dozen types to choose among,
And always one of them would be as like
As he'd have made it had he worked from life.
Or liker, maybe, since from practicing
He'd got the habit of their bodies down
And worked a few improvements year by year
He'd not have had the skill for, standing there
Before a live impatient fidgeter.
(The subjects were a blur, and he was lost
Did he not know beforehand how they'd look.)
In better days, he'd add a Chinese bowl,
A globe, a lamp, so one could recognize
One thing, if not the sitter, from the house.
That done, he'd feel no qualm to use again

That very pose next door. Those were the days,
When he'd more work than he could keep apart
And strangers would discover they were kin!
Now that was over with, and thin enough
The last few years, what with these picture-men
And his fingers' treason, never warm again,
And lately this immense fatigue and sleepless
Worry. There wasn't need for him these days.
But somehow other painters made their way.
The better ones, perhaps. For them at least
There always would be portraits, but no more
The easy work, the one day masterpiece
His clientele could just about afford.
It wore him down. He scratched a living out,
At making portraits in the hinterlands
That took him far too long, and brought him less
Than once he might have got for ready-mades.
Sometimes he worked at landscapes, having seen
How slovenly the panoramas looked
Before the candid lens. But every one
Turned falser at his hands than he had meant:
Each pasture turned to Pasture, each barren ridge
Of rusty traprock into Majesty,
Each town to Yankee Trader with His Wares.
The thought of them revolted even him
Who'd learned the hard way not to make too much
Of what he'd only call his art to those
Who'd pay for it, never to himself.

His one self-portrait, made at twenty-two
—A solid month he'd peered into the glass,
A new black frock he never wore again
Chafing his neck each time he raised an arm—
Showed him at strict attention in the shade
Just at the point of turning to the light
That slanted through the murk into his face,
One eye in dark, the other tense, acute.
He'd caught his breath, as if impatiently
Peering after something still unseen
That might be just emerging through the dense
Entanglement of shadows he himself
Had only barely parted, his glossy hair
Involved in that obscurity that spared
One hand, and an expectant silent glare.
His palm was down, the slender pointed brush
Slanting upward, vivid in his grasp,
Poised to take his will, the fingers bending
Firmly, and just this once correctly drawn.
The face was wrong, though: smooth and juvenile,
A clear pale forehead, almost featureless.
And though his mouth was pursed for concentration,
His lips were full and pink, his cheeks as rosy
As an infant's. Even round that waiting eye
The face was soft, as if it would be plump.
His candor here's what made a fool of him.
He finished up the painting in a rage,
His final touch a faint, ironic dimple
In the face he couldn't make himself keep straight.

He knew too well just how he saw himself,
And what he was, rebuking even then
The vanity of thinking he had failed.

Now Peterson was staring in mid-stride
And Hunter fumbled in embarrassment—
"Excuse me, could you say that once again? . . .
All right. I'll do the painting. At your price."

II

She never sat like that, in stiff amaze
Unsteady on the edge of, yes, it must be
That chair by the fender, but only she,
He saw, could be betrayed in just that way.
It was a graceful girl's awkwardness,
Her shy obedience before that stranger
Who stood behind the tripod, stern, unseen,
Demanding and mysterious as a priest.
She held a formal pose he'd used, himself:
The face in three-fourth's view, the right hand curving
Palm down on the table at her side
In emblematic ease and unreserve,
The left hand resting calmly in the lap
She'd never quite smoothed down, the best black dress
Too stiff to seem that it belonged to her,
And on her face that look of good behavior
And discomfort, grimly keeping still
To almost please that tense, exasperated

Man at the machine, who'd only smile
A little after the exposure time.

Hunter knew a dozen types of stark
Alert rigidity before the lens.
It is her goodness, not timidity
Before that bullying, that makes her stiff.
Perhaps she even pitied him, the ass,
As if by bearing with him she'd invent
Some manners for him, if he'd take the hint.

She wasn't trying to be reticent
But how can one be natural by main force?
"How should I sit?" he overheard her say
To the photographer, polite and shy,
And Hunter knew she'd be the same with him.
Oh, she would be a good girl to the last
And slip them all, herself no less than them.
What would she want? What Hunter'd want her to.
But what he wanted was for *her* to want
Some thing he hadn't thought of in advance.

And then he heard his own voice, tactfully
Assuring her she looked just fine to him
As plausibly as he knew how to sound.
Relax, his voice went on, just be yourself,
The one thing you can never simply be!
He heard the eager thin encouragement
He knew she'd not believe, nor meant her to,
Since her slight wariness would be herself,

An air of hesitant flirtatiousness
A part of his *metier*, of course, as was
The certainty that neither meant it, quite,
That hint of eros nudged to courtliness
A make-believe in which one's style of play
Showed how one was, or could be, anyway.

One has to be more tactful with the dead.
That's what would save him, if he would be saved.
He would have watched her wondering how to sit,
And made a guess, as she composed herself,
How he'd compose for her what she believed
She might have come to, could he puzzle out
As far as he'd the patience to. (Impatience
Was his vice, he saw, not flattery:
The smiling masks he painted were as far
As he dared trust himself to go. Beyond
Might be themselves, or just impertinence.)
Were she alive, she would have taken up
His view of it, and that would be the end.
Despite himself, the photographer at least,
In rushing like a Vandal after her,
Had done a kind of justice to her flinch.
How hard she'd tried to do her best for him.
That, not her reluctance, caught his eye.
She knows how poor a thing that picture is,
And hates herself for her rigidity,
And knows herself—Hunter, marveling,
Stepped back before the flash of the idea
(What kind of ass I've been to think the good

Buy goodness with stale sweet stupidity!)—
And knows how poor a chance she squanders here
Yet plays the wager out as cool and sure
As if it weren't the only one she had.
She almost shakes with what she cannot do:
I am like this. I am. That's all I am.
And while we're smiling at her awkwardness
She's burned her ships as we will never do
(And all we'd wondered was if she'd keep still
For us). Why should she "be so good" for us?
For someone else, someone in the room
And not the daguerreotypist after all?
For Peterson perhaps? Her father's girl
Just as she looked before she left the house
On someone's arm? But why the touch of fear
That makes her stiffen her unsteady hands?
She thinks she'll wrong him somehow, leaving him
Alone in this big house with nothing more
Than—ah!—and from the mantle looking down
He saw a slender woman dressed in white
That swept like water from her lifted arm,
A sketchpad in her hand, her pale fine hair
Loose in the style of twenty years before
About her eager mocking merry face—
That picture of his wife. Long dead, I guess,
And somewhere far from here. *I* wouldn't dare
Give any woman such a face, at least,
Or such a dress. Then suddenly he knew
She'd painted it for him herself, the minx.
And then had died just when the girl was born,

Or else old Peterson would have no use
For that beau bully with his camera.
Yes. She must be just her mother's age.
It is his way of wishing her farewell.
Her? Yes, both of them. The one to death,
The other to—She doesn't know, herself,
And that's what she's afraid for here, not him,
But for that other man unknown to her.
And *that's* for whom she's trying to be so good.

It was too much for the photographer,
That goodness. And Hunter knew that even he
Would find that goodness armed at every point,
Forgiving him that fool design on her
She never would believe he didn't have.
Or didn't he? He couldn't face it down.

He turned his mind to those broad stripes of dark
He had been spreading out, half-absently.
Yes, that will do. No need for furniture,
Unless a hint of table for her hand.
I'll use a straighter chair, unseen except
In how her dress will fold. He blocked it in,
Quick swathes of black descending in a swirl,
A branch of sleeve to where the table'd be.
The pale and cloudy oval of her face—
She'd turn her head to look straight from the frame,
Her body just a shade inclined away,
As if left to herself she would look down
At that left hand she didn't know where to put.

He wondered why he fussed so much with it,
When for the moment it would paint itself,
His brush not needing him until at last
He'd have to turn his mind to those details
He hadn't had the skill to carry off
When at his best, much less the last few years.
He might as well have kept his mittens on
When it would come to painting. But for now
He should be daubing on with half a mind,
Not finicking away the easy part.
It was her goodness worried him with his.
God save him, did he wish, at this late date,
To make her goodness just a road to his,
His breaking through, his sense of his career,
Since Goodness naturally would lead to Art,
Which he would gratefully ascribe to her,
And maybe tell himself was not his own,
His eye alone on justice done to her.
Mysterious, the mighty works of love.
Better botch it now than fake it later.
The eyebrow that he drew was slightly raised.

You seem to think me very breakable.

"I'm trying not to think of anything."

I see that you are courtly with your subjects.

"I'm sorry. I didn't mean that as it sounds.
I mean a painter shouldn't think too much

Or what he paints is only what he knows
Too well already to take pleasure in."

You mean you're trying not to think of you . . .

"And not succeeding. It's a kind of pride."

And so is that. Now I'm the forward one!
But tell me, Mr. Hunter, why you think
I ought to be afraid of what you do.
You think I hate to have my portrait done?
In fact, I'm very grateful to you now
For any kindness you have shown my father.
This painting will be his. The picture's not.

Hunter caught his breath. "Not his?"
                                        Of course.
He'd planned to have a double portrait done.

"Of you and him?"
                   Of him?
                              "O.K., I see.
The one he took the picture for, not him."

My cousin Andersson. You've heard the tale?

Hunter couldn't say just what he'd heard
But made a leap, "You knew his name, but never
Saw his face, not even in a picture—"

Not then, although I saw him soon enough.

He heard her rueful smile. "This picture, then,
Was Peterson's idea, an offering?"

And a betrothal gift.
     "Ah, my dear!"

No, you are mistaken. I'd no doubts.
Not then, nor after.
     "But you're doubting now."

No. But if I'd doubted then, I'd be
Alive to doubt. Doubt is a little thing.

"Ah . . ."
   Wait. You make me rush ahead too fast.
He was a nice young man I might have loved.

"You *might* have loved . . ."
      He could have shot himself.
—How could he talk like this?—and looked away
To steal a second for his dignity,
But heard her draw a breath: she thinks I know
Just what I'm doing here—she'll see it through.

I hadn't time, you see, not then.
      She took
Him at his word, he saw. And saved them both:
She has to know it through. It's all she has.

"Not then, but later on."

What did I know?
I'm sure my father never thought to see
The daguerreotype again.

"He'd sent it off?"

To Sweden, yes. For Henryk, don't you see?
My aunt had planned to send his picture back,
But Henryk came himself, all in a rush.
And that was just our luck, as it turned out.

You're wondering how I'd tie myself for life
To someone whom I'd only heard by name
In someone else's letters?

"Shouldn't I?"

I didn't. And I've often wondered why.

"I'm quite at sea, Miss Peterson, but not
So lost as not to hear in what you say
—And might I say, surprisingly?—just what
You don't regret, don't even wonder at.
It is a kind of bravery, I see,
Explains how you might wed this man on just
Your father's say so, and a wistful hope
That not all life escapes you heedlessly.
It also makes you speak so free with me
And makes me dare to be the same with you
Although my trade survives by courtesy . . ."
He worked a fluted collar for her throat,

The embroidery reflecting back the cool
Clear stream of winter sunlight to a face
As pale and lucid as the winter sun.
She laughed at him.
                              That isn't in the plate.

"I haven't painted one in years."
                                        Outmoded?

"No. Just haven't made the time. Or no,
Don't have the hands these days to do it well."

I wish I'd had a dress so fine.
                                        Inspired,
He loosely drew a sash about her waist
Of silky tulle.
                              You flatter me, I see.

"I'd like to, if I had the skill. But tell me.
You learned to love this boy from overseas.
That's no surprise to me. But where is he?"

She had a pause. *I thought you knew it all.*
She paused again, quite at a loss for words.
He was already ill when he arrived.

"And you took death from him!
                                        I didn't know!
Now what a fool I've been: I didn't hear
A word your father said. He must have thought

When I said nothing back, I hated him,
And blamed him just as he must blame himself."

That's why he trusts you'll paint this picture well.

"I couldn't work that way."
                              I understand.
Still, you've got him wrong. He's not the fool
You take him for, or hasn't always been.
Poor man, he thought he'd got away from death.

"So it was grief that made him cross the sea.
You were a little child."
                              We came alone
And he'd left everything behind but that.

"The painting. Yes. I thought so."
                              There were more.

"There'd have to be. She's better than I am.
All right: he thought he'd bring himself to life
Again, by living here—God, what a place!—
I guess he thought death wouldn't know the way!
And got his foothold here, his castle built,
But didn't marry, though I'm almost sure
She told him to. That's why he never would."

All right. Go on.
                              "But missed his land and kin,
More every year as you were growing up,

And couldn't wed you to some Ashfield boy."

Oh, no. I hadn't even looked at them.
I knew since I was small whom I would wed.

"A boy you'd half made up—your father's tales,
Letters in a tongue you didn't know . . ."

Not so. I knew it well.
                    "But didn't write
Yourself—there I'm not wrong—until the way
Was cleared by others who'd approved of all
The plans."
                    That's how we do it, Mr. Hunter.

"He was your mother's nephew, and you saw
Right on that wall just how he'd have to be:
A larger life than Ashfield had to show.
So, proud and lonely, still a foreigner,
You bet it all upon a fantasy."

Now, Mr. Hunter, life is small enough.
I understood how vague my notions were.
But which are not? I knew it was a risk.

"But here's what you don't say—I see it now—
How you could put that foolishness aside,
And pity him. You do so even now,
Despite it all. You'd do the same again
Though he brought nothing to this house but death."

Oh, no. That isn't all. I thought he'd be . . .

"A handsome stranger!"
                              But he was a boy
Of just my age. A gentle, thoughtful, boy.

"That wasn't your idea."
                              It was the gift
I hadn't thought of: all his gentleness.
I didn't know until just then that what
I'd thought of love was wrong. But that was right.

"Ah, my dear . . ." But that was all he said.
He'd raised the color in her cheek a bit,
And gave a hectic glitter to her eyes.
Her gaze is clear and perfectly composed
But bright, mysterious.
                              I place it now.
You've made the painting later.
                                        She had a pause.
Yes. That night again. We'd buried him
Just days before. And then I woke and knew.

Hunter raised his brush and held it in the air.
You're right. It could be only then. Oh God.
And she was horrified. *I see. I see.*
I knew just what was coming, all of it.
I couldn't face it down. I kept it back.

Yes. That's right.

But I can't help you there.
I just can't bear to go through that again.
Forgive me, Mr. Hunter.
            Then, nothing.

III

He'd filled the lamp again, and stared an hour,
Shading his eyes against the frozen glass
And watched the wind-surge, thrashing in the dark,
And every cry and every blast of sleet
Shook the sash and banged the shutters back.
He stood there at a loss, while day dragged in,
The color of his breath upon the pane.
At last he saw the empty branches plunging
Meaningless in panic in the pale
Tormenting endless frigid rush of rain.
Behind him, where he could not bear to look,
His painting waited, tremulous and warm
In the yellow sphere of lamplight, almost done.
It wasn't right. He hadn't had the skill.
Yet gave up to the task more than he had.
He hadn't wanted anything enough
Except to shake away that clinging, stale
Discontent with nothing he could name.

Suppose that he had loved her? Would she live,
Transfigured by a pure and upright force
That he had never had? He'd made her up.

But if he hadn't, had the living girl
Sat there before him, shy and secretive,
He'd never have been brave enough, or cruel,
To see what she had seen unflinchingly,
And show it back to her, reflected there
In that clear light of her untroubled gaze.
She saw precisely what she wouldn't show:
She shielded her poor father from the truth
She'd want him to be sure she'd seen beyond
Before she'd let him see it. Hunter saw:
It hadn't made the slightest difference
Except to him, perhaps, who made still less.
Oh, stupid heart, when will you feel the sting!
Then suddenly he saw her in the glass
As she had been the very night before
He'd set the painting, how she'd coughed awake
And felt her skin on fire, and lit the lamp
To see there in the mirror the tell-tale face.
Long, how long, she watched it watching her,
Then shook her head, and with a rueful laugh
Snuffed out the light. Hunter took his brush
And on her hand he put a golden ring.
He saw her puzzlement: "It's not for me,"
He said aloud, "It is for Andersson,
The only gift I have the power to give.
I've had to give you up. How hard that is,
God only knows. But you yourself have taught
Me how it can be done, and for that gift
God bless and keep you in His love and mine.
The ring's my best. Look down at it sometimes."

$$\overline{V}$$

$$\equiv$$

Starbuck's Watch

Over the swell, heeling across its back,
The smooth ship skating down aslant,
The helmsman holds her steady past the hard
Shimmer of the moon on distant crests.
The light translates itself, follows the eye.
A golden road he races, shivering
With the clean forgetfulness of mariners
Whose vanities the waves have rubbed away.

He pinches himself awake, thinks of his wife
Asleep in the chilly house, the stirring child
Who will be born before he comes to port,
Remembers the sand-blown streets of Edgartown,
Sea-grass, kelp-rack, driftwood, anything
But the moon, and the wakeful one who set it there.

The Phantom Arm

FOR RON COX

It was not a dream. Baffled and stubborn,
It was pain's sophistry: *It's all a lie.*
There's nothing lost at all. You understand?
The motion where nothing moved, the burning itch
In no fingers, the doorknob cold and solid
Turning in no hand—No, he said,
It is my senses, taunting me with loss.
At least he wouldn't be deceived, and wasn't.

And yet it was still there, when twenty years
Had rubbed it clean of pain. Upon his chest,
It lay as last he saw it whole: it was
Itself, no more, not the mute, unreckoning
Reproach of flesh, but body's history,
The facts that tender us the body's world.

At Mount Pleasant

His Daughter
1973 Lauren Elizabeth 1990

Every day, on her way from work
She waits there half an hour at the curb,
A well-dressed woman in a small blue car,
Looking at that stone beyond the grate,
As if calm at last, as if self-possessed at last,
As if to comfort, not be comforted.
Today I saw her kneeling on the grass,
Setting a chrysanthemum in place,
A hopeless gift. She wore a broad straw hat
Like any woman in her own back yard.
Task done, she sat back on her heels and smiled.
I almost caught her eye. I wanted to.
But I walked on past. I couldn't bother her,
Nor tell her how I'd watched her keeping watch.

Parking Downtown

The sunlight clattering in the windy lot
Half full of cars, their blazing chrome and glass
The idiotic echo of that sun,
The brown grass clinging, brittle to the roots
And drier than the sand it huddles in,
You tell yourself (snapping fast your lock)
The mind is its own place, the only place.
And on the stoop, their golden heads bent down,

You see two bright-haired kids, breath held, behold
A Queen-Anne's-Lace reaching up in bloom.
Today it is a flower. Another day
They'll rip it from the ground, but for today
It is a flower. Don't say it isn't. Don't say
It's just a flower because they think it's one.

Charles Capers

(ST. HELENA ISLAND, S.C., 1815)

Impatient at the ferry slip, he hoped
He'd long be out of Beaufort when they heard
The fool he'd been, the fools he'd made of them,
Who, with their greetings neatly written out,
And their proffer of the finest house in town,
Had rushed to Charleston, puzzled, but "prepared
To show what grace St. Helena can show
For one whose name alone made kingdoms fall."

St. Helena, it seemed, was somewhere else.
A heron beat across the steaming marsh.
He heard each rush of wings, so still the air,
And saw, where willows bent, the blur of white,
And saw the flash of hoes among the fields
Where all the bolls were bursting like small bombs.

The Rake's Progress

All flesh is grass, O gorgeous girls, all flesh.
Avid, arid, mortal beauty, mute
Insistent quivering thing, if for an hour
I turned me dizzy in the spinning world,
Thrust this in that, thumbed my nose at time,
Repeating myself into immortality, know
That worn out and detumescent, I called my art
The glands' memento mori, and betook

Myself unto philosophy, sang hymns,
Read sacred books, and thought upon my death.
And the spirit burned with the urgency of flesh,
But, lacking flesh, was not consumed. The body
I have spent was mine to spend; this unspent
Angel's robe was frayed before my birth.

The Immortality of Poetry

If someone reads this, love, when we are dead,
It won't be us who live again, not you,
But she, some other she, and in my stead
Some other man will wrap, the way I do,
Firm arms around her shoulders, kiss her throat,
Blow back her hair to kiss her ear, her brow,
And hear her catch her breath, that clear, soft note,
And kiss her parted lips (as I do now).

If halting, half-afraid, they get by heart
The terms of love they copy down from us,
Will we, through them, somehow learn the part
We had to improvise and bluster through?
If through us they find out the stern, mysterious
Secrecies of love, will we know too?

The Personal Memoirs of U. S. Grant

Cancer-choked, he sat on the porch and wrote.
They'd hauled him in his chair to some resort
For "Fresh Mountain Air, and no Mosquitoes."
He was a sideshow to the scenery.
The crowds would wait to watch him from the fence
And spend their change on knickknacks from the store.
Each afternoon they had a bulletin:
"Normal stools today and no blood coughed."

Cancer-choked, he sat on the porch and wrote
No puling exculpation, nor blasts of brass
That men might kill for or be happy dead.
The blood and fraud were past. He let them lie.
Clear-eyed and spent, he wrote down what he knew
As if his honesty itself were hope.

Little Girl Alone with Doll

The doll was the first to inflict upon us that tremendous silence (larger than life) which later kept breathing on us out of space, whenever we came to the limits of our existence. — RILKE

No matter what, she gives her that same smile,
But what she's smiling at she doesn't say.
She knows the words a six-year-old would know,
And speaks when spoken to, in a changed voice.
"I love you, Janey. Say it: I love you."
And so she does. Still, there is that smile.
Then she's crushed against a streaming face.
"Just tell me everything will be all right."

But it won't be, and that won't matter either,
Not to that smile, past caring and past hope.
The girl has made a place for her; she waits.
Calm, breath held, all done with lying now,
She sits there ready, watching for the one
Who never speaks, whom still we're waiting for.

Of the Surrender to Sleep

"Even my poor virtues keep me awake.
Reasoning with God in a puny voice,
I count them over and over, a string of beads,
The gold I buried so as not to lose.
Had my sins been bolder, I would know
How pure the wrath of God, how clean the flame
That burns me clean, refines me to myself:
At least I'd know myself for what I am."

You cannot free yourself from will by will;
You just get weary of it, wear it out,
And something happens you weren't counting on.
You do not go to sleep. You lose your way.
It will not matter if you get there now:
You were not going anywhere but here.

My heart cries out to you and cries out.
At my rising up from bed, at my work,
At drawing to the table to eat,
At conversation with my wife or with my friends,
At waking in the silence of a summer night
All at once I cry out to you,
Spring in the desert, breath to the fainting,
How long, oh out of reach yet ever near, how long?

Notes

"Love and Fame" is set on the night Keats wrote the sonnet "When I Have Fears."

All of the events (including the dream) of "Night on the *River Queen*" are taken from accounts of Lincoln's visit to Richmond the week before his assassination.

The title of "Common Ground" alludes to the J. Anthony Lukas book about racial conflict in 1970's Boston, although the conflict in the poem is not specifically racial.

"Thomas Chaplin" and "Charles Capers" refer to incidents in Chaplin's diary, republished by Theodore Rosengarten in his book *Tombee*. Charles Capers really did get up a greeting party to meet Napoleon, unaware that the St. Helena Island he was being exiled to was not the one in South Carolina.

The *Californian* was the ship that, because its radio operator was in bed, did not respond to the distress calls of the sinking *Titanic*.

Viglius Zuichemus was a real person, and the poem follows an actual letter to Erasmus.

In "Elizabeth Keckley" I have followed, although altered a little, her own account in *Behind the Scenes*.

The dirigible accident alluded to in "1938" actually took place several years earlier. (There is famous newsreel footage of the event.) I have changed the date to allude to the Munich Pact.

Acknowledgments

"Viglius Zuichemus" appeared in *Salmagundi*.

"Love and Fame" appeared in *Yale Review*.

"Starbuck's Watch" appeared in the *Formalist*.

"The Phantom Arm" appeared in *New Letters*.

"Night on the River Queen," and "What Ellen Said" appeared in *Southern Review*.

"Sapphics," "Ice Storm," "Charles Capers," and "Mary's Gift," appeared in the *Paris Review*.

"Barren Season" appeared in *Western Humanities Review*.

"Anna Peterson" appeared in *Southwest Review*.

"Work without Hope" appeared in the *Journal*.

"The Match" appeared in the *Greensboro Review*.

"Aboard the *Californian*" appeared in *Webster Review*.

"The Personal Memoirs of U. S. Grant" appeared in *Kansas Quarterly*.

"Little Girl Alone with Doll" appeared in *America*.

Poetry Titles in the Series

John Hollander, *"Blue Wine" and Other Poems*
Robert Pack, *Waking to My Name: New and Selected Poems*
Philip Dacey, *The Boy under the Bed*
Wyatt Prunty, *The Times Between*
Barry Spacks, *Spacks Street: New and Selected Poems*
Gibbons Ruark, *Keeping Company*
David St. John, *Hush*
Wyatt Prunty, *What Women Know, What Men Believe*
Adrien Stoutenberg, *Land of Superior Mirages: New and Selected Poems*
John Hollander, *In Time and Place*
Charles Martin, *Steal the Bacon*
John Bricuth, *The Heisenberg Variations*
Tom Disch, *Yes, Let's: New and Selected Poems*
Wyatt Prunty, *Balance as Belief*
Tom Disch, *Dark Verses and Light*
Thomas Carper, *Fiddle Lane*
Emily Grosholz, *Eden*
X. J. Kennedy, *Dark Horses*
Wyatt Prunty, *The Run of the House*
Robert Phillips, *Breakdown Lane*
Vicki Hearne, *The Parts of Light*
Timothy Steele, *The Color Wheel*
Josephine Jacobsen, *In the Crevice of Time: New and Collected Poems*
Thomas Carper, *From Nature*
John Burt, *Work without Hope*

Library of Congress Cataloging-in-Publication Data

Burt, John, 1955–
    Work without hope : poems / by John Burt.
        p.   cm.
    ISBN 0-8018-5371-0 (alk. paper).
    I. Title.
PS3552.U767W67   1996
811'.54—dc20

95-43088